Twins Mac & Madi Get Sporty Coloring and Activity Book

By Linda Herron

Illustrator Marie Delon

Twins Mac & Madi Get Sporty: Coloring and Activity Book

DEDICATION

"May you love your similarities, express your differences and enjoy your friendship."

This coloring and activity book helps twins work through what activities they would like to participate in as individuals and twins.

What are your names?

Your name: _____

Your twin's name: _____

Draw yourselves!

4

Mac and Madi signed up for swim lessons.
Mac and Madi always did everything together. *Everything.*

What sports & Activities Do You Like?

Your name: _____

I like:

1 _____

2 _____

3 _____

4 _____

Madi and Mac joined gymnastics.

They tried ballet too.

Madi spun left.

"I don't like ballet!" Madi professed.

What
Sports & Activities
Did You Try?

Your name: _____

I tried:

1 _____

2 _____

3 _____

4 _____

What
Sports & Activities
Did You Try and Like?

Your name: _____

I liked:

1 _____

2 _____

3 _____

4 _____

What **Sports & Activities** Did You Try and Dislike?

Your name: _____

I disliked:

1 _____

2 _____

3 _____

4 _____

Hmmm... we may like different activities?

They tried cheerleading.

The team kicked left. Mac kicked right.

The team did tucks. Mac did buckets.

Regrouping

Deciding

What Sports & Activities Do You Still Want To Try?

Your name: _____

I would like to try:

1 _____

2 _____

3 _____

4 _____

Soccer or Tennis?

The girls couldn't agree. Because they do "EVERYTHING" together! Deciding different activities?

Maybe they try something...
...DIFFERENT?

Will You Choose DIFFerent
Sports & Activities Than Your Twin?

Your name: _____

I choose:

1 _____

2 _____

3 _____

4 _____

Will Your Twin Choose DIFFerent Sports & Activities?

Your Twin Name: _____

I Think They Will Choose:

1 _____

2 _____

3 _____

4 _____

Happy!

Madi chose soccer.

Mac cheered Madi on from the sidelines.

The illustration shows a sign reading "GO #10!"

Madi was happy!

Mac chose tennis.

Madi cheered from the sidelines.

Mac was happy!

Mac and Madi could do different things.

Draw You and Your Twin Doing SOMETHING DIFFERENT:

Draw You and Your Twin Doing Something Together:

Mac and Madi still liked to do lots of things together...
just not everything.

About the illustrator

Marie is a Mexican illustrator based in the city of Puebla, Mexico. Her work includes mostly digital techniques and mixed media. In the past, she has worked for independent publications and zines, children books and advertising, both national and international. Marie is a full-time graphic designer and implements her illustrations in her daily job.

Recently she's been working on personal creative projects that include character design, merchandising design and concept art for video games. When she's not designing, Marie loves watching movies, reading comic books and playing tabletop RPG games.

About the Author

Born and raised in Rhode Island, Linda Herron knows firsthand what it is like to grow up as an identical twin. In fact, the most wonderful part of her childhood was spending time with her best friend and twin sister.

Because Linda recognizes the unique bond—and the unique challenges—that being a twin entails, she was inspired to create a series of children's stories about being an identical twin. Her book series name is Twins Mac & Madi.

When she isn't writing children's books, Linda spends some of her time writing business articles and blogs. As a Financial expert, she provides strategic advising that transforms businesses by boosting profitability. Her financial advice has been featured on media outlets including American Express, LendingTree, and Daily Business News, and she holds a bachelor's degree in accounting from Bryant University.

Today, Linda lives in California and enjoys the sunny, seventy-five-degree weather every day. Though her twin still lives in Rhode Island, they visit each other to spend time together.

If you'd like to learn more, purchase books, or join her mailing list, you can connect with Linda via her website www.lherron.com or her Instagram, Facebook, and Twitter accounts.

Note from Publisher:

We hope more than anything your twins enjoyed this book. If they did please consider leaving us a review on Amazon. It only takes a few minutes, but it would be so much appreciated. Reviews really help the Author, and it helps potential customers know about the book.

We also would like to create more content for twins to enjoy so it would be incredibly helpful to hear what parents are wanting to read with their twins.

If you have any feedback for us, then we would love to hear from you.

Email us at: Linda@BigLittlePress.com

www.ingramcontent.com/pod-product-compliance
Lightning Source LLC
Chambersburg PA
CBHW041002170626
46815CB00002B/112